THE TWIDDLE TWINS' AMUSEMENT PARK MYSTERY

by HOWARD GOLDSMITH

illustrations by CHARLES JORDAN

For my mother, Sonia, in loving memory—H.G.

For LeeAnne and Paden—C.J.

Text copyright © 1998 by Howard Goldsmith
Illustrations copyright © 1998 by Charles Jordan

For information contact:
MONDO Publishing
One Plaza Road
Greenvale, New York 11548

Visit our web site at http://www.mondopub.com

Designed by Christy Hale
Production by The Kids at Our House

Printed in the United States of America
98 99 00 01 02 03 04   9 8 7 6 5 4 3 2 1

Library of Congress Cataloging-in-Publication Data
Goldsmith, Howard.
    The Twiddle twins' amusement park mystery / by Howard Goldsmith ; illustrations
by Charles Jordan.
        p.   cm.
Summary: When Tabitha Twiddle carelessly leaves her beloved toy hippo Blippo in a
playground sandbox, she and her twin brother must retrace her steps to find him.
    ISBN 1-57255-618-8 (pbk. : alk. paper)
    [1. Lost and found possessions—Fiction.   2. Twins—Fiction.   3. Toys—Fiction.
4. Amusement parks—Fiction.   5. Hippopotamus—Fiction.]
I. Jordan, Charles, ill.   II. Title.
PZ7.G575Tt   1998
[E]—dc21   97-42316
                                                              CIP
                                                              AC

Contents

Where is Blippo?

"Have you seen Blippo?" Tabitha
Twiddle asked Timothy, her twin brother.
"Why, is he missing?" Timothy asked.
"Of course he's missing," said Tabitha.
"Otherwise I wouldn't ask you."

"Where did you leave him?" Timothy asked.

"If I knew that, I wouldn't be looking for him," Tabitha answered sadly.

"Let's look for him together," Timothy suggested. "Did you look in the bathroom? You always leave your toys there."

They ran to the bathroom. Blippo wasn't there.

"Where can he be?" Tabitha cried.

"Did you look in your toy box?" asked
Timothy.

"Of course I did. That was the first
place I looked," Tabitha answered.

"Well, let's look again," said Timothy.
They ran to Tabitha's toy box. Blippo
wasn't there either.

They looked under Tabitha's bed.

"Come out, come out, wherever you are, Blippo!" Tabitha called.

"Blippo can't understand you," said Timothy. "He's only a toy hippo."

"Blippo is real to *me*," Tabitha said.

They searched all the rooms of the house. Then they looked in the attic and the basement. No Blippo.

"He's gone forever," Tabitha sobbed.
"I'll never see my Blippo again. Come
back, Blippo!"

Buried Treasure

Timothy thought hard.

"Did you play outside in the yard today?" he asked Tabitha.

"Yes," Tabitha answered.

"Come on! I bet we'll find Blippo there," Timothy said.

But Blippo wasn't in the front yard.

The twins ran around to the back of the house. Clarabel was curled up under the porch.

"Clarabel!" the twins cried together.

Clarabel sprang to her feet.

"Here, Clarabel," Timothy called. "Did you take Blippo to play with?"

Clarabel glanced from Timothy to Tabitha and from Tabitha to Timothy. Then she took off like a shot.

"Come back, Clarabel!" Tabitha called. "You haven't done anything wrong. Just show us where you put Blippo."

Clarabel circled the house five times, with Tabitha and Timothy right behind her. Finally Clarabel ran into the house.

"Maybe she buried Blippo the way she buries her toy mouse," Tabitha said. "Poor Blippo. Buried alive!"

Timothy and Tabitha began digging up
the backyard. They found Clarabel's rubber
mouse, a flea collar, a tangled ball of
yarn, six fish bones, and five empty cat
food cans. But no Blippo.

"Here's my magnifying glass!" Tabitha
yelled.

"And my old sneakers!" Timothy
exclaimed.

But still no Blippo. Where could he be?

Poor Blippo!

"Let's put our heads together," Timothy said.

Tabitha bumped heads with Timothy.

"Ouch!" Timothy exclaimed. "I meant let's put our heads together and *think*. Where did you go this morning?"

"I know!" said Tabitha. "I went to the playground."

"Let's go!" Timothy cried.

In the playground Tabitha and Timothy looked by the swings. They looked under the slide. They looked on the seesaws. They looked all over. But there was no sign of Blippo.

"I remember now!" Tabitha cried.
"I left Blippo in the sandbox."

They ran to the sandbox. It was
empty—except for some footprints.

"Look," said Timothy. "Here are
Blippo's footprints in the corner. See
his four little toes?"

"I forgot to take Blippo home with me," Tabitha said, close to tears. "I just left him here, poor thing. Poor Blippo. He's an orphan now."

"Don't cry," said Timothy, trying to comfort her. "Someone probably found him. Let's ask in the playground office."

"Sorry, nobody turned in a toy hippo," said the playground director.

Tabitha was broken-hearted. She turned to leave with Timothy.

"Wait," the director said, calling them back. "Come to think of it, I did see a girl playing with a toy hippo."

"Where?" Timothy and Tabitha asked together. "What did she look like?"

"She was over near the sandbox. But I don't remember how she looked," said the director. "I was too busy to pay attention."

"Think!" Tabitha pleaded. "Pleeease!"

The man thought hard. "Sorry, that's all I can tell you."

"Thank you," said Timothy and Tabitha. Disappointed, they left the office.

Checking the Rides

On their way out of the playground,
Tabitha and Timothy met their friend
Daisy.

"Daisy, I lost Blippo," Tabitha said.

"But *I* found him—in the sandbox,"
Daisy said.

"*You* found him?" Tabitha shouted, jumping up and down excitedly.

"Yes, I was holding him for you," said Daisy.

"Oh, thank you, thank you!" Tabitha cried. "Where is he?"

"Well, umm. That's the problem. I lost him, too," said Daisy with a weak smile.

"What! You *lost* him?" Tabitha and
Timothy exclaimed. "WHERE?"

"I think I left him at the Amusement
Park," Daisy answered.

"Let's go find him," said Tabitha,
pulling Daisy and Timothy by their hands.

When they reached the Amusement
Park, Daisy looked around, puzzled. She
scratched her head. Where had she been?

"Did you go on any rides?" Timothy
asked.

"I went on the Merry-Go-Round.
Maybe I left him there," Daisy answered.

They bought ride tickets and hopped on the Merry-Go-Round. Around and around they whirled. But Blippo wasn't on the Merry-Go-Round.

Next Daisy headed for the Roller
Coaster. She jumped into the front car.
The twins hopped in, too.

Up, down, up, down went the Roller
Coaster at lightning speed. But Blippo
wasn't on the Roller Coaster either.

Daisy ran down the boardwalk to the Bumper Cars. Tabitha and Timothy followed close behind. They all jumped into bumper cars, searching for Blippo.

CRASH! BAM! went the cars, spinning off each other with loud bumps. Round and round they spun. But Blippo was nowhere to be found.

The Giant

Daisy and the twins staggered off the Bumper Cars.

"I'm dizzy," said Timothy.

"Me, too," said Daisy.

"Who's dizzy?" asked Tabitha, nearly falling over.

Tabitha was eager to continue the search. "Did you go anyplace else?" she asked Daisy.

"I know! I went to the Hall of Mirrors," said Daisy. "But I got scared and ran out."

"You might have left Blippo there," said Tabitha.

They bought tickets and ran into the
Hall of Mirrors.

One mirror made them look tall and
thin.

"Hey, skinny," Tabitha said to Daisy.
"Look at you!"

Another mirror made them look short and fat.

"See that," said Timothy. "We look like bowling balls with legs."

And another mirror made them all look tiny and wavy.

"Look!" Tabitha suddenly cried. "A giant! Over there!"

Timothy jumped back. Then he looked again. "That's not a giant," he said. "It's something in a mirror."

Tabitha looked carefully. "It's a giant Blippo!" she shouted. "Blippo is the giant in the mirror."

Daisy and the twins ran over to the mirror. As they stepped in front of it, they became giants, too.

And at their feet stood Blippo. He looked as if he were staring straight at the mirror.

Tabitha picked up Blippo and gave him a big hug. "Oh Blippo, I missed you," she said.

"Hip, Hippo, Hooray!" squeaked Blippo as Tabitha squeezed him tightly.

As Timothy, Tabitha, and Daisy left the Amusement Park happily, Clarabel ran up to them. Clarabel was playing detective, too. She had followed them all the way to the Amusement Park.

"Clarabel," Tabitha and Timothy exclaimed. "We found Blippo!"

Clarabel jumped up and licked Blippo's face.

"Clarabel thinks Blippo is *her* toy," said Timothy, laughing.

"HIP, HIPPO, HOORAY!" Blippo squeaked again.